Why do kangaroos only live in Australia?

T0364512

Written by Susannah Reed

Illustrated by Joseph Wilkins

Collins

What's in this book?

Listen and say

desert

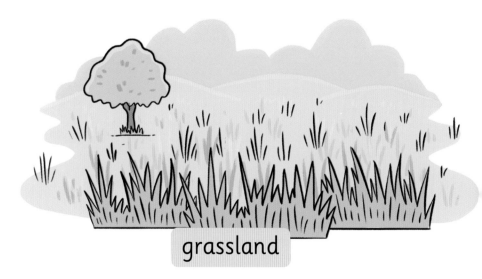

grassland

mountains

forest

🎧 Hugo was in the park with his cousin, Vicky.

"Look, Vicky," said Hugo.
"Is that a kangaroo?"

"Don't be silly," said Vicky.
"Kangaroos don't live in our country."

"Kangaroos only live in Australia," said Vicky.

"But why?" asked Hugo. "Why do kangaroos only live in Australia?"

"Let's see," said Vicky.

Australia is an island. It is the biggest island in the world.

It has lots of towns and cities. Sydney is the biggest city.

Australia is a very dry country. It has mountains and deserts. It has grasslands and some forests, too. And it has lots of animals and birds.

Kangaroos live in grasslands and forests.
They eat grass, flowers, leaves and insects.

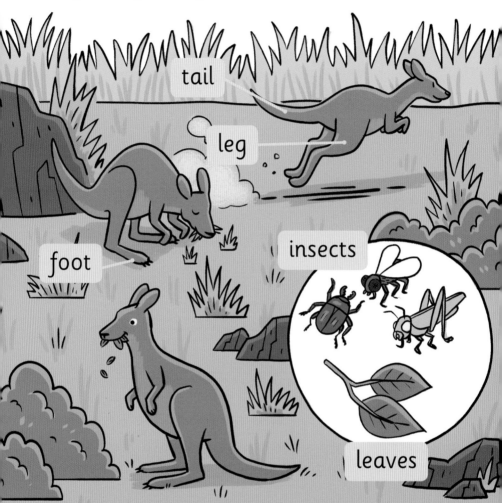

Kangaroos have strong legs, big feet
and a long tail. They can't run but they
can jump!

This is a mother kangaroo and her baby.

pouch

Mother kangaroos carry their babies in a pouch. The baby is safe here in its mother's pouch. Can you see it?

What other animals only live in Australia?
This is a koala. Koalas live in Australia.
A mother koala carries her baby in a
pouch, too.

eucalyptus

koala

Koalas live in eucalyptus trees. They eat
the leaves from the tree. Eucalyptus trees
grow in Australia.

A mother wombat has a pouch, too.

wombat

Wombats live under the ground in grasslands and forests. They eat grass and plants.

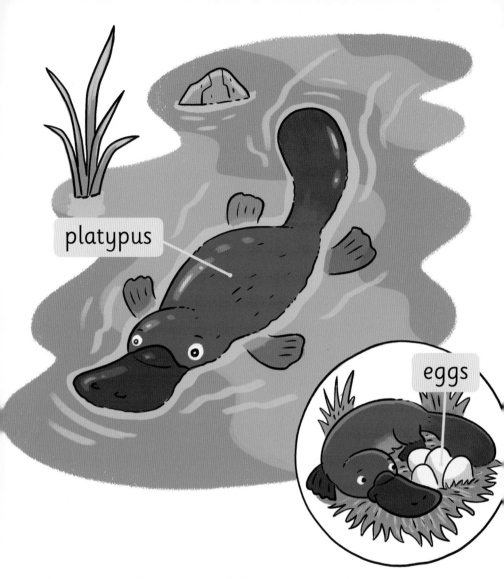

platypus

eggs

This is a platypus. Platypuses live next to rivers. They swim and they eat insects and small animals. Platypuses aren't birds, but they lay eggs.

The echidna is a small animal. Echidnas live in many different places in Australia. They live in mountains, forests, grasslands and deserts. Echidnas lay eggs, too.

echidna

Emus are the biggest birds in Australia. They have green eggs. Emus can run, but they can't fly.

emu

A kookaburra is an Australian bird, too. Kookaburras make a funny noise. They laugh!

kookaburra

All these animals only live in Australia. Why?

This is an island. An island has water around it.

Australia became an island millions of years ago.

The animals in Australia were different to animals today. These animals only lived in Australia. Why? The sea stopped them going to other countries.

After millions of years, animals change.
Australian animals changed, too.

Some of the animals were very big!
Can you see big kangaroos, wombats
and koalas? Can you see big birds?

19

These animals changed into the Australian animals and birds we see today.

And that's why these animals only live in Australia!

"Wow!" said Hugo. "I love Australian animals. I'd like to go to Australia!"

"Me, too!" said Vicky.

Picture dictionary

Listen and repeat

echidna

emu

kangaroo

koala

kookaburra

platypus

pouch

wombat

1 Look and match

has a pouch

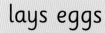

lays eggs

2 Listen and say

Collins

Published by Collins
An imprint of HarperCollins*Publishers*
Westerhill Road
Bishopbriggs
Glasgow
G64 2QT

HarperCollins*Publishers*
1st Floor, Watermarque Building
Ringsend Road
Dublin 4
Ireland

William Collins' dream of knowledge for all began with the publication of his first book in 1819.

A self-educated mill worker, he not only enriched millions of lives, but also founded a flourishing publishing house. Today, staying true to this spirit, Collins books are packed with inspiration, innovation and practical expertise. They place you at the centre of a world of possibility and give you exactly what you need to explore it.

ISBN 978-0-00-839842-2

Collins® and COBUILD® are registered trademarks of HarperCollins*Publishers* Limited

www.collins.co.uk/elt

British Library Cataloguing in Publication Data

A catalogue record for this publication is available from the British Library.

Author: Susannah Reed
Illustrator: Joseph Wilkins (Beehive)
Series editor: Rebecca Adlard
Publishing manager: Lisa Todd
Product managers: Jennifer Hall and Caroline Green
In-house editor: Alma Puts Keren
Project manager: Emily Hooton
Editor: Barbara Mackay
Proofreaders: Natalie Murray and Michael Lamb
Cover designer: Kevin Robbins
Typesetter: 2Hoots Publishing Services Ltd
Audio produced by id audio, London
Reading guide author: Emma Wilkinson
Production controller: Rachel Weaver
Printed and bound by: GPS Group, Slovenia

MIX
Paper from responsible sources

FSC
www.fsc.org

FSC™ C007454

Download the audio for this book and a reading guide for parents and teachers at www.collins.co.uk/839842